# Other Titles by TW Brown

## The DEAD Series

DEAD: The Ugly Beginning
DEAD: Revelations
DEAD: Fortunes & Failures
DEAD: Winter
DEAD: Siege & Survival
DEAD: Confrontation
DEAD: Reborn
DEAD: Darkness Before Dawn
DEAD: Spring
DEAD: Reclamation
DEAD: Blood & Betrayal
DEAD: End

## The New DEAD series

DEAD: Onset (Book 1 of the New DEAD series)
DEAD: Alone (Book 2 of the New DEAD series)
DEAD: Suffer the Children (Book 3 of the New DEAD series
DEAD: Don Evans Must Die (Book 4 of the New DEAD series)

# Zomblog

Zomblog
Zomblog II
Zomblog: The Final Entry
Zomblog: Snoe
Zomblog: Snoe's War
Zomblog: Snoe's Journey

## That Ghoul Ava

That Ghoul Ava: Her First Adventures
That Ghoul Ava & The Queen of the Zombies
That Ghoul Ava Kick Some Faerie A**
Next, on a very special That Ghoul Ava
That Ghoul Ava on the Lam
That Ghoul Ava On a Roll
That Ghoul Ava Sacks a Quarterback
That Ghoul Ava has an Appetite for Deception

# Grim Grimoire:

# Witchy Woman

TW Brown

I am here to share a special secret.
Monsters are real.

Monsters held a very special place in the heart and mind of TW Brown. From nightmares to friends and even superheros. I hope you enjoy following his journeys into the Grim Grimoire.

# 1

Sometimes the monster wins. Most people don't believe that monsters exist. Monsters are wrong. They have become the subjects of countless movies and books. Vampires. Werewolves. Zombies. Witches.

Where did those ideas come from? Did they just magically appear on the scene? Perhaps you think they were created by the imaginations of a few talented (if not misguided) writers for the sheer thrill? No.

Oh my beloveds, I am here to share a special secret. Monsters are real. Yet, somewhere along the way they stopped being scary. I blame the man with the fedora and the bladed glove. I believe you know him as "Freddy" the homicidal standup comedian. Rest assured my beloveds…monsters are seldom funny.

You might be thinking to yourself, "How do you know?" Well, I must confess to you here that I am, in fact, a ghost. Yes, a ghost writer.

Since my death, (a messy incident involving an early printing press of all things) I have roamed this world. I have in fact met many of the inspirations for what was once deemed gothic literature. Now, it seems "gothic" equates to pale skinned undernourished, angst-ridden humans who favor dressing in black and discovering new body parts to pierce. Most of these 'wannabe' corpse imitators would wet themselves if ever they came face-to-face with a real vampire. In fact, the black would come in hand to cover the stain that would appear in their pants.

If I may, for a moment, I would like to talk about a certain monster. A witch actually. Not the harmless, nature loving, Wicca type witch. No my beloveds, I speak of one of the

# CHAPTER ONE

true Queens of Evil. An honest to goodness, potion brewing, black cat petting, Hansel and Gretel eating, witch.

Oh I'll bet many of you were told the Hansel story with that phony happy ending. I assure you that the bedtime story you were told as a child is quite false. The Grimm Brothers changed the ending after being visited by the woodcutter's wife (actually a second cousin to the gingerbread house witch). It seems that shortly after that particular tale was published she was forced to go in to hiding by certain self-righteous villagers with a literal axe to grind.

After promising that the Grimm's would meet a considerably worse fate, they rewrote the ending. Of course the poor woman had to remain in hiding but with the less gruesome ending that included the children returning to their father nobody much cared about hunting her down and dishing out some form of retributionary punishment. Sadly, she emigrated to America and found a home in Salem, Massachusetts. How was she to know that being able to swim was a skill first honed by witches and warlocks?

I would like to share a story about a witch I know. She goes by the unlikely name of Elizabeth Breyer. I could tell you many frightful tales about that relatively young lass. I will enjoy the thought that hearing this tale might make some of you squirm. You see, my beloved, this in not the movies. Sometimes… the monster wins.

So, welcome to Miss Breyer's eighth grade classroom. Room 317. It looks like any classroom you have ever sat in. At the head of the five rows that contain six student desks each, sits a heavy wooden teacher's desk. Somewhere under the clutter and only slightly organized chaos is a placard with the name "Miss Breyer" engraved.

The mess is quite normal. Elizabeth Breyer is not a very organized witch. Clever? Yes. Evil? Indubitably. Organized? Absolutely not. On that desk, under the clutter, is a seating chart. A square for each desk in each row. A name in each square for each student in each desk. In the second row, in the third desk is the name "Troy Matthews". A little black star is next to that name. We will get to that in a minute or two.

As for this classroom, there are the usual rows of books, mostly encyclopedias. Hanging over the erase board behind the teacher's desk are the world map, US map and a projector screen. Like I said, this classroom is much like any other classroom you've been in. The one thing that might make this classroom a bit unusual is the raven perched on its stand in the corner near the desk. The raven is named 'Anabel Lee', but will only answer to that name if spoken by Miss Breyer.

Over the years some students have made the mistake of calling that infernal bird a crow. They are always corrected. First by Miss Breyer.

"Anabel Lee," Miss Breyer will say, "Are you a crow?"

Then by the obsidian bird itself.

"Raven!" Anabel Lee squawks in her croaking bird voice.

With a slight cock of its head, Anabel Lee fixes one yellow eye on the poor student who misspoke.

"R-r-r-raven."

All the students at Dairy Glen Middle School quickly learn who Miss Breyer is. Rumor around the school is that she is a witch. Most of the boys in school argue against this point.

"She don't look like no witch!"

"Witches don't have long blonde hair!"

"Sabrina did!"

"That was a stupid television show."

And so the arguments go. Nobody ever wins or loses because after all, how can one really tell if a person is a witch? Some can swim. Some can't. Few people realize that the skill, while introduced by witches is not inherent to all of them. In addition, I've never met any person who didn't burn. Those folks in Salem went about it all wrong. You see, there is a special code of conduct for witches. Rule number one says quite simply, "If asked directly under no threat or duress if you are a witch, you must answer truthfully and directly." Most people do not know that rule. In fact if you should meet a witch now, please do not mention that you heard that bit of information from me.

Any old way, as you will eventually discover for yourself, I tend to wander off my subject rather frequently. So, without further delay, back to Miss Breyer. Nobody is really certain of her age. Another trait of a true witch is that they age different from regular folks like you. Truth is, (and I have this on excellent authority – from Anabel Lee actually) she is a youthful eighty-two. However, the normal guessing range usually falls between early 30ish to mid 40ish. Some of the bagboys in the market even offer up "not a day over 30!" That makes Miss Breyer smile sweetly and tweak their noses which in turn makes the aforementioned bagboys blush brightly in their cheeks.

"How does she doe it?"

"What is her secret?"

That is what some of the teachers ask. That is also something they would be very upset about if they learned the real truth. You my beloved, are about to learn not only her beauty secrets but much more. Oh so much more. So, check under the bed and make sure the windows are locked. After all…sometimes the monster wins!

.

# 2

Troy Matthews was just about as scared as he had ever been. I can't say it was the scariest moment of his young life though. That actually comes a little later in the story. Miss Breyer stood up at the dry erase board with her purple marker in her hand, her piercingly predatory eyes scanned the room.

Something about Miss Breyer did not sit right with Troy Matthews. He glanced around the classroom at some of the other kids. They all seemed interested in the volume problem being explained on the board. Mostly.

Troy could feel Billy Skalden, the weird kid that sat right behind him was staring into the back of his head. He felt a strange tingle in his stomach every time "Fishface" looked at him. The nickname sure fit. Billy Skalden had buggy eyes that almost seemed to bulge from the sides of his way to meaty face. His thin-lipped puckered mouth always made it seem as if he were either whistling or gasping for air like one of those mud fish you could catch at Dorsey Creek in August. But the creepy thing was Billy's skin tone. It was a pasty white that looked as if it could turn moldy green if given half the chance.

"Please don't let her call me!" Troy prayed silently to the unseen forces that watched over twelve-year-old boys who are not very good at "solving for X."

"Troy." Miss Breyer smiled. She smiled that very same smile that the cartoon Grinch smiled right after he figured out that his little dog would be the perfect reindeer to haul his sleigh. In other words a very scary smile.

The sudden tap on his desk made him jump in his seat. He looked up into the cold gaze of Miss Breyer. Her golden eyes seemed to look at him like he managed a bird might look at a fat juicy worm.

"Perhaps you can tell us the answer to the question on the board Mister Matthews?" Miss Breyer's voice had a certain playful tone to it. It was sort of how a cat might bat around a little mouse before biting its head off.

So much for that unseen force that watches over twelve-year-old boys who are not very good at 'solving for X'. He stared at the blue marker that Miss Breyer held out to him. It may as well of been a poisonous snake or a big hairy tarantula.

He tried to swallow the lump that seemed to suddenly sit right in the middle of his throat. There were a number of bad things about this current situation. The first and foremost was that he would be standing in front of the entire class demonstrating that he had no hint of an idea how to 'solve for X'. Next, there was Anabel Lee on her perch giving that glare that burned right through your skin. Last of all, there were the two skeletons suspended on their stands. A man and a woman.

Did I forget to mention these? Well, let me correct that oversight. On each side of the eraser board is a skeleton on a blue stand. These are used during health, science, and biology. They smell…odd. Aah! Since we are on the subject, on a small stand nearby is another skeleton. The plaque says simply "CAT".

Anyways… back to our boy, Troy. There he stands staring up at the board. His insides twist and turn until he is almost certain that his generic frosted flakes will come up. The equation is like a seamless knot that seems to offer no insight as to how it should be solved. Something about, "If a grave is dug six feet deep, seven feet long, and three feet wide and X the volume of the grave, write as an equation and solve for X." I bet you would do much better than our young lad, Troy.

Sadly, he stood at that board for what seemed to be almost forever. Try as he might, he just didn't understand algebra.

# CHAPTER TWO

Troy gulped once and tried to answer. Nothing came out except a timid croaking noise that in no way resembled his voice. A tittering of laughter managed to overcome the pounding heartbeat filling his ears. However, glancing around, Justin saw mostly the knowing looks of pity. Nobody in Miss Breyer's sixth grade class liked being the sole focus of her attention.

Finally, though not mercifully, Miss Breyer asked Troy to return to his seat. A couple of the kids snickered behind their hands. Mostly everybody just felt sorry for him. They knew what was coming next.

"Mister Matthews," the teacher's voice was just above a whisper, yet it seemed to hammer at his ear drums with each syllable. "You will be staying in from recess. Perhaps I can conjure up a couple of remedial problems that will bring you up to speed with the class." A sigh rippled through the room. Most of the children had not even realized they were holding their breath.

"Yes ma'am," he slid down into his desk. His stomach twisted further into several quite uncomfortable knots.

A collective gasp echoed in the class. No punishment could compare to staying in from recess, unless it was staying in from recess and spending the entire period doing math under the eye of Miss Breyer.

With a sharp pivot on her pointy toed black shoes, Miss Breyer returned to the board. Click. Click. Her shoes seemed to be on the verge of igniting sparks as they struck the dull gray linoleum. All eyes followed the teacher now. For as much as even his best friend Wally Tucker might feel bad for him, nobody wanted to join Troy in his punishment.

Trying desperately to concentrate on his math book the feeling that someone or something very bad was watching, churned in his stomach. It was worse than that feeling when the basement light would flicker off at home sometimes. Or even worse, the time he and Wally had snuck out late one night to explore the old, abandoned house at the end of Wally's street.

# CHAPTER TWO

Every footstep seemed loud enough to be heard for miles. The scratching and scurrying on unseen creatures, Wally insisted they were only rats seemed to come from all directions. Then they had stumbled upon the sleeping wino.

Wally had actually tripped over the winos legs and sprawled across the floor of what had probably been the dining room. They had run so fast that night. Sometimes Troy swore he could smell that rotten sour stench that had filled his nose the night when they met the wino. He could still hear the slurred voice calling "Come back boys, we can get to know each other better!" And then there was that gurgling wet cough ridden laugh. Troy shuddered.

Glancing around hoping that everybody was still focused on Miss Breyer and her math problem and not the fact that he could not seem to sit still he locked eyes with Fishface. For the first time, Troy realized what it was about Fishface that gave him the creeps.

He never blinked. He just stared at you with those dark empty unblinking eyes. No expression on his face. Just sitting there staring at Troy and totally creeping him out. Well, he thought to himself, maybe Old Fishface would like some of his own medicine. He glanced up at Miss Breyer. She was busy scribbling something on a notepad on her desk.

With a sudden turn of his head, Troy snapped around and stared with his best wide-eyed glare. Fishface just stared back at him. His expression never changed from that glazed over dull-witted look that seemed to keep permanent residence on his face.

"Mister Skalden perhaps you can show the class, in particular our Mister Matthews, just how this equation is solved." Although she was addressing Billy Skalden, her eyes never left Troy's. Her thin lips peeling back just enough to flash pearly white teeth.

A slight rustling sound came from the desk directly behind Troy's. Billy Skalden sat in the fourth desk in the third row. Billy Skalden is what most kids might call "weird" or perhaps "creepy".

Now might be a good time to explain a couple of things that most of the other students at Mountain Top Middle School already know about Billy Skalden. He was never a very good student. Even that is being a bit kind. In fact, just last year he failed the eighth grade. This is his second year in Miss Breyer's class

He use to be quite the bully but now he is strangely quiet according to most of the boys in school, only when Billy is not around just in case it is all a trick of some sort, he is called a "Big Wuss". His other most notable difference is that he tends to smell rather disgusting. Sort of like a tuna fish sandwich that was left out in the sun on a July day. In other words Peeee-Yewwww!

The most common observation about Billy Skalden is that he 'just ain't right'.

There are a few things that are merely your typical school-yard rumors regarding Billy as well. You see, for as long as most of his classmates have known him, Billy Skalden was one of the elite players of the gym class classic, Dodge Ball. He threw round rubber missiles of death. If his eyes locked on you, there was usually an evil gleam accompanied by an I'm-gonna-cream-you-and-there-is-nothing-you-can-do-about-it smile. His specialty was called the 'Ankle-Breaker'. This particular shot of his would fly at its victim scant inches above the glassy looking gym floor. It would strike at about ankle level and upend the hapless target. You did not want to be the last member of the opposing team. The Aknle-Breaker was automatic as the game-ender. To add insult to injury, nobody had ever thrown a ball he couldn't catch. Billy Skalden had the only undefeated Dodge Ball record in known Mountain Top Middle School history.

That was until last year. After missing a week of school he returned, and it seemed at first that maybe he had suffered some sort of head injury. He talked a little slower and was even worse in his schoolwork than before. But the day everyone remembers to this very day is when Beatrice Magillacuddy caught a Billy Skalden Dodge Ball throw!

That moment, the entire gymnasium went silent. Even Coach Creswell's jaw hung open in silent amazement. What made the event final in every body's mind was what happened next. Jeremy Wigglesworth pushed his glasses up on his nose and in his single shining moment that would live on in nerd notoriety, he lobbed one of his typical weenie armed throws. That red rubber ball just seemed to drift through the air like a perfectly spherical balloon for forever. It struck with a barely audible THWAP on Billy's cheek then bounced harmlessly to the gymnasium floor. Billy was out.

To you, my beloved reader, that may not seem too incredible. Rest assured, however, that the news was shocking enough to be recounted in the austere confines of the faculty lounge. Truly this was an amazing event.

Additionally, there were several incidents that began to be noticed, Billy was no longer bullying the sixth grade. That, in and off itself was like the earth leaving its orbit of the sun. In fact, he just seemed to drift along the hallways of school. If he spoke, which was almost never, his voice was flat and odd like the generated voice from that old Speak and Spell toy.

Now, Billy Skalden walked up to the board. As he passed, his hand brushed Troy's. Cold. Troy glanced up and for just a brief second their eyes met. It really was like looking at one of those dead fish in the display case at the grocery store. Yet, for just a brief second, he saw…what? Fear? Pleading?

The skin on Troy's arm suddenly bubbled up in a million billion little goose bumps. The back of his neck prickled with what felt like tiny electric shocks. Something was very wrong with Billy Skalden.

Troy watched with an almost hypnotized fascination as the once feared bully of Mountain Top Middle School sort of stumble-walked to the front of the class. With a peculiar awkwardness, he groped for the marker held out by Miss Breyer. In jerks and starts, like a strobe light was prompting each motion, Billy wrote out the equation

$$6' \times 6' \times 7' = X$$

$$X = 105^3 \text{ feet}$$

"Excellent work, Mister Skalden," Miss Breyer seemed to beam at her student as if he had just defined Einstein's theory. "Now, hand me the marker and return to your desk."

Doing exactly as he was told, Billy Skalden now trudged back down the aisle of desks. This time he looked straight ahead and seemed to be unaware of anything around him.

Strange. Troy shrugged and then picked up his pen to copy the problem on the board. He knew there was probably a very simple solution to this stupid algebra he thought to himself. But darn if it didn't escape him for the moment.

The rest of the class seemed to fly by. You know how when you are having a lot of fun with your friends and all of a sudden it is time to go home? Well, it was sort of like that for Troy except without any of the fun. The next thing he knew, it was recess.

The bell rang and Miss Breyer gave her dismissal. Everybody dashed for the door. Well, everybody that is except for our poor unfortunate lad, Troy Matthews. A few of his friends gave a look of commiseration. That is to say that, while they certainly felt sorry for him, they absolutely would not want to take his place.

Eventually the last student slipped out the door. It happened to be Billy Skalden. He glanced back at Troy and for the second time their eyes met. There was something there. Almost like Billy wanted to warn him of some unspeakable horror but was too horrified himself to speak. Something unspoken passed between the boys in that moment.

# CHAPTER TWO

"You can go to recess now, Mister Skalden," Miss Breyer spoke without looking back as she erased the board. It was as if she could see behind herself...

With a click of the door, they were alone. Teacher and student. Hunter and prey?

Grim Grimoire: Witchy Woman

# 3

"So Mister Matthews" Miss Breyer leaned back against the corner of her desk, her shiny red fingernails clicking on the lacquered pine surface. "Do you want to tell me what was so interesting that you did not feel the need to pay attention in my class?"

Troy wondered if this was how the mice that were fed to the snake in Mr. Friday's sixth grade class felt right before being swallowed alive. Those creepy eyes were worse than Billy's. Miss Breyers eyes burned a hole in you. They could incenerate a lie before it fell off your tongue. The gold flecks in her iris' seemed to dance like a shaken snowglobe.

"I dunno," was the best he could manage and that came out in a choked whisper.

"That is hardly an answer, Mister Matthews." Pushing off from the desk she walked to the door that opened out to the main hall of the school building. Glancing both ways as if making sure nobody would see what sorts of unthinkable horrors she was about to commit, Miss Breyer pulled the door shut. There was something filan in the way the latch clicked. Troy began to wonder if he would survive recess and see his friends ever again.

Turning abruptly on her heel she stalked the edge of the classroom. As she began to speak, it reminded Troy of the way a tiger prowls in its cage at the zoo. "You seem to make it a habit of ignoring my lessons, Mister Matthews. You disrupt my class with whispered jokes and rude noises. Do you want to end up taking my class again next year?"

The thought of another year with Miss Breyer caused an involuntary shudder. Troy fidgeted at his desk as she seemed to

# CHAPTER THREE

glide towards him without touching the floor. He rubbed at his eyes with clenched fists. It was only then that he realized his fingers were cramping because he had them digging into his palms. Opening his hands he didn't need to look to know there would be four half moon shaped spots in each palm where his fingernails had cut into tender flesh.

She leaned down close to him and it was almost enough to bring tears to his eyes. Never before had Troy been so completely frightened. Scared was not a good enough word to describe the feelings that had his stomach churning and his bladder squeezing so tight he felt like he would wet his pants any moment. He could smell her breath. It was a mixture of something cinnamony and something else. That something else was bitter and if evil had a smell, Troy was certain this was what it would smell like.

Looking into those golden eyes, he noticed some very strange and unsettling things. Up close those golden eyes seemed to swirl with colors. Not regular colors either, the gold was like the metal of his mothers wedding ring. Definitely not normal.

Now my beloveds, this is probably a good time to explain that a real live witch is very unlike the cartoons. In fact that movie "the Wizard of Oz" only gets it part right. A true witch is a ruthless creature that assures her well-being above all others.

They do not twitch their cute little noses and cast all manner of spells. Spells are actually an extremely complicated matter and the slightest mistake can cause a terrible backfire. They alter what already exists or rob from one source to feed another. For instance, a witch could cast a spell to make you lucky at games of change, but your hair and toenails would fall out.

Why, I know of this one witch down in the swamps of the Florida Everglades. She spent three weeks preparing a spell for a customer that would place an incurable sickness on an

# CHAPTER THREE

enemy. One of the ingredients was a taste bud from a guppy. By accident, she mixed in a taste bud from a puppy.

Imagine her customer's surprise when his very worst enemy suddenly discovered the ability to mysteriously pick the winner of any sort of race. Cars, horses, people, it made no difference. As if that were not enough, the customer was cursed with everything he ate or drank tasting like grilled liver. It was a most unfortunate incident indeed.

I also find it very tedious, all these so-called "new-age" witches. Chant a few lines under the moon and everybody wants to call themselves a witch! How absurd is that? Real witches first and foremost do not advertise. Nor do they spend time in each others company. There were too many competitive and egotistical issues for that.

Oh terribly sorry. I tend to wonder at times. I can be going along just fine as frog hairs with a tale and before you can say "Jack Robinson!" I'm off and running on a subject completely unrelated to whatever it was I was so meticulously documenting only a blink-of-an-eye before.

Of course poor Troy answered in a meek and tiny voice that he very much did NOT want to repeat Miss Breyer's class! Then he stumbled and fumbled at a way to say he meant nothing bad about Miss Breyer.

Eventually recess was over, and the desks filled with flush faced children. Well...except for Billy. He looked and smelled very much as he always did. Class resumed as always and when the final bell rang, Troy was first out the door.

At the bicycle rack, Troy's circle of friends gathered around to hear the gruesome (and highly exaggerated) tale of what took place during his unfortunate detainment.

"Did she threaten to turn you into a frog?" Jeremy Wiggleworth asked with a wide-eyed seriousness.

"Did Anabel Lee perch on her shoulder and stare at you?" Brian Thompson shuddered.

# CHAPTER THREE

"Do you think she cast a spell on you?" Stevie Reynolds whispered, taking a step back as if he expected Troy to explode or burst into flames.

"No," Troy leaned close to his friends over his bike. "But I did notice that her eyes seemed to like...change colors when she bent real close like."

His friends glanced at each other with doubtful and almost disappointed looks. Then being the swell bunch of fellas that they are, they each made poor excuses and hopped on their bikes to pedal off in their separate ways.

"Well it is much creepier if you see it for yourself" Troy muttered to himself.

It was at that moment that young Troy came up with the worst idea of what would be a short and unfortunate life. He would spy on Miss Breyer and catch her in one of her witchy things.

Witchy things?" Hey, it's his idea, not mine. Did I mention that our young Troy is not the cleverest of lads? Well I've certainly implied it!

Anyways, as he pedaled along…the idea seemed to just shape itself rather nicely and tidily. So begins the beginning of the end.

# 4

Now I believe I mentioned a little black star next to young Troy's name on Miss Breyer's seating chart.

Troy had no way of knowing that he had been selected as special on the night of the parent-teacher conferences the second week of school. His fate was actually more the fault of his dear mother. Oh! Also Sherri Matthews' boyfriend, Harold "call me Uncle Hank" Babbs.

You see, I've mentioned the unnaturally youthful appearance of the lovely Miss Breyer. What I have not been forth coming about is that she actually steals her youth. Yes! From the children in her class! Where else could she find such a splendid and never-ending supply? Isn't that just so wickedly delicious? I told you witches can alter things but must steal from one source to shape the other. I guess plastic surgeons do much the same thing when you really think about it.

You see, each year during the first teacher conference she hand picks her "winner". It is a very simple process. A newcomer is often her first choice simply because nobody would miss them if they disappear. Think about it. Most likely in your own classrooms there is that creepy weird, new kid. Would you miss them if they were gone tomorrow? Not bloody likely!

The most difficult part of her plan is to get rid of the family that the child belongs to. That takes a little more work and effort. That is why during the conference she pays close attention to the parents of any possible candidate.

Believe it or not, there are grown-ups that can vanish with out anybody even noticing. Oh, it's true! In fact, Miss Breyer would tell you herself that she is actually doing the community a great service.

# CHAPTER FOUR

Now take Billy Skalden for instance, a bully with no redeeming qualities. His dad was the town drunk and his mom was not much better. Why even their pet cat had a poor disposition. Now they are actively involved in furthering the education of many young children. Just not in a conventional way. Not only that but they have never been so close to young Billy. They are daily witnesses to his progress in school. Oh! And they are a great deal quieter these days.

You see, when Miss Breyer met Billy's mom, she went against her normal ideas of selecting a newcomer. Between her smelly cigarette breath and the unidentifiable chunks of food wedged between yellow teeth, she knew that this woman's absence would be noticed. But it would hardly be missed. Plus, she was very aware of Billy's reputation as a school bully.

Now before you go and put some good and noble crusader label on Miss Breyer, understand that she does what she does for on e reason and one reason only: Personal Benefits. Her own health and well-being is first and foremost in her mind.

Also, as you will soon discover, her method is less than pleasant, and truth be told she enjoys the pain and torture she inflicts on her victims. I do believe that I warned you that this story can be unpleasant. Well, it is about to begin in earnest so now would be a good time to turn on an extra light, check the doors and windows to be sure they are locked, and make sure your little brother or sister is no where around where they can sneak up and yell "BOO!!"

# 5

Troy peddled his bicycle down the street that would eventually bring him home. He suddenly jammed on his brakes skidding to a tire screeching stop. There was no way he could just let Miss Breyer get away with this! She had embarrassed him in front of the whole class.

There just had to be a way he could make her pay. In that moment he began to get an idea. It was a wonderful, spiteful, and in his case unfortunately a final idea. He would kidnap Anabel Lee!

A crooked grin spread across Troy's face as he pushed off and began to pedal home once more. He would need to come up with a bit of a plan. On the rest of the way home that plan slowly but surely unfolded in his mind.

In the history of really bad plans this one was fated to end up in the "Bad Plan Hall of Fame" if indeed such a place existed. Now you will be tempted to yell out "Don't do it!" or some such warning. Rest assured it is far too late for that. I am relating to you a story that has already transpired. It would be like me yelling, "Don't do it!" about something you were punished for three weeks ago. You would look at me like I as crazy.

Anyway, once he got home. Troy ran upstairs to his room. Closing the door he breathed a sigh of relief. No sign of his mom or 'Uncle' Hank. Tossing aside his books, he walked over to the big aquarium that took up the whole top of his dresser. Coiled in one corner was his pet boa constrictor.

"Hi Ya Snakey!" Troy tapped on the glass. Yes I know, not a very original name.

"Bout time for another mouse eh?"

# CHAPTER FIVE

Snakey flicked his little forked tongue as to say "Why yes it is!"

Flopping down on the bed, Troy allowed his mind to consider his plan. He felt certain that it was fool proof. If that were the case, our poor boy is worse than a fool.

Before long, it was dinner time. It was at dinner that Uncle Hank announced that he had been downsized at his latest job. Downsized of course is Uncle Hank's way of avoiding the word 'fired'. He's been "downsized" a lot.

After dinner, Troy's mom and Uncle Hank sat down on the couch and turned on the television. Within a couple of hours they were both slumped in opposite corners with loud rattling snores drowning out the TV.

Scrambling up the stairs, Troy began to put his plan into action. Now I must warn you that any plan so hastily put into play will almost certainly lead to disaster. When making a real plan, you must consider at least three things going wrong, then, count on two things you never imagined also going wrong.

Putting on his black jeans and a zip-up black sweat jacket, he slipped downstairs to the kitchen. Under the sink with all the cleaning stuff were the yellow rubber gloves he used when washing the dishes. Troy knew from all the police shows on TV that nobody would find your fingerprints if you wore rubber gloves. Stuffing them into his pocket, he slipped out the back door. Hopping on his bike he began his fateful journey to Miss Breyer's house.

You may be curious as to how Troy knew where his teacher lived. I'm sure many of you have teachers you do not quite like, yet you have no idea where they live. Well, due to her scary reputation, lots of kids knew where her house was. It is the local Haunted House. Now I'm certain all of you know where the Haunted House is in your neighborhood, right? I thought so.

So, into the night he pedaled. Every set of approaching headlights sent him darting down a side street or into the nearest set of bushes. It seemed as if the distance to Miss Breyer's house had quadrupled.

Finally, he turned into the dark cul-de-sac where her house was located. Carefully he hid his bike in some nearby trees, pointed outward so that if he came running back he could jump on and be away in a flash. Putting on the rubber gloves, he snuck along in the shadows.

This might be a good time to tell you that it was the night before Halloween. To some of you that might not seem such a big deal. To most of you it is simply a night of knocking on doors, getting candy, and doing annoying pranks to people you do not like. To Miss Breyer, it is the most important night of the year.

The sound of the recess bell made him jump. All the kids stuffed their books under their seats in the little cubby hole that was supposed to hold all their school stuff.

A few looks of sympathy were flashed at him as all the kids of Miss Breyer's sixth grade class made a dash for the door.

Fishface smirked!

**The growing voice in horror
and speculative fiction.**

Find us at www.maydecemberpublications.com
Or
Email us at twbrown.maydecpub@gmail.com

TW Brown is the author of the Zomblog series, his horror comedy romp, That Ghoul Ava, and, of course, the DEAD series and the New DEAD series. Safely tucked away in the beautiful Pacific Northwest, he moves away from his desk only at the urging of his Frisbee catching Border Collie Tyrion, or one of his Newfoundlands, Freyja or her younger sister Loki.

He plays a little guitar on the side...just for fun...and makes up any excuse to either go check on his beehives or strolling along his favorite place...Cannon Beach. His hobbies include training his Newfoundlands to be show dogs working on their championships, water rescue working on their WD titles and draft carts working on their DD titles. And we should never forget to add his African Greys named Sheldon, Lisa, and Paul. He answers all his emails sent to twbrown.maydecpub@gmail.com and tries to thank everybody personally when they take the time to leave a review of one of his works.

He can be found at www.authortwbrown.com. The best way to find everything he has out is to start at his Author Page. You can follow him on twitter @authortwbrown and on Facebook under Author TW Brown, and also under May December Publications.